WEATHER REPORT

Wordsong

BOYDS MILLS PRESS

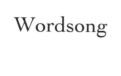

Illustrated by

Annie Gusman

WEATHER REPORT

POEMS SELECTED BY

JANE YOLEN

Published by Wordsong
Boyds Mills Press, Inc.
A Highlights Company
910 Church Street
Honesdale, Pennsylvania 18431

Publisher Cataloging-in-Publication Data
Main entry under title.
            Weather report : poems selected by Jane Yolen ; illustrations
by Annie Gusman.—1st ed.
[64]p. : ill. ; cm.
Includes index.
Summary: An anthology of poems covering all types of weather and seasons.
ISBN 1-56397-101-1
1. Weather—Juvenile poetry. 2. Seasons—Juvenile poetry. [1. Weather—Poetry.
2. Seasons—Poetry.] I. Yolen, Jane. II. Gusman, Annie, ill. III. Title.
808.81—dc20   1993
Library of Congress Catalog Card Number: 92-81075

First edition, 1993
Book designed by Joy Chu
The text of this book is set in 12-point Cochin.
The illustrations are done in mixed media, including cut paper and acrylics.
Distributed by St. Martin's Press
Printed in Mexico

10   9   8   7   6   5   4   3   2   1

Due to space limitations, permission to reprint previously published material may
be found on page 60.

For LILIAN MOORE, she knows why,
and with special thanks to LINDA MANNHEIM

WEATHER REPORT

Pointer in hand,
the weatherman stands
before the map.
"Here," he says,
tracking a thunderstorm.
"There," he says,
predicting fog.
"Forty percent,"
figuring snow squalls.
"A low, a high. . ."

But above us, the sky,
with a logic all its own
announces sun.

—Jane Yolen

ON LITTLE CAT FEET: Fog

ONE MISTY MOISTY MORNING

R A I N

Rain before seven
Quits before eleven
—Country wisdom

CHATTERBOX, THE RAIN

Bursting with news,
Chatterbox, the Rain,
Talks all day
To the windowpane,

To the trash can lid
Rattles on and on,
Babbles this and that
To the backyard lawn,

Chatterbox, the Rain,
Talks and talks all day,
And *still* has puddles
And puddles to say.

—*Beverly McLoughland*

RAIN IN SUMMER

How beautiful is the rain!
After the dust and heat,
In the broad and fiery street,
In the narrow lane,
How beautiful is the rain!
How it clatters along the roofs,
Like the tramp of hoofs!

How it gushes and struggles out
From the throat of the overflowing spout!
Across the window pane
It pours and pours;
And swift and wide,
With a muddy tide,
Like a river down the gutter roars
The rain, the welcome rain!

—*H. W. Longfellow*

RAIN SIZES

Rain comes in various sizes.
Some rain is as small as a mist.
It tickles your face with surprises,
And tingles as if you'd been kissed.

Some rain is the size of a sprinkle
And doesn't put out all the sun.
You can see the drops sparkle and twinkle,
And a rainbow comes out when it's done.

Some rain is as big as a nickel
And comes with a crash and a hiss.
It comes down too heavy to tickle.
It's more like a splash than a kiss.

When it rains the right size and you're wrapped in
Your rain clothes, it's fun out of doors.
But run home before you get trapped in
The big rain that rattles and roars.

—John Ciardi

APRIL RAIN SONG

Let the rain kiss you.
Let the rain beat upon your head
    with silver liquid drops.
Let the rain sing you a lullaby.

The rain makes still pools on the sidewalk.
The rain makes running pools in the gutter.
The rain plays a little sleep-song
    on our roof at night—

And I love the rain.

—Langston Hughes

HOPI PRAYER

Come here, Thunder, and look!
Come here, Cold, and see it rain!
Thunder strikes and makes it hot.
All seeds grow when it is hot.
Corn in blossom,
Beans in blossom,
Your face on gardens looks.
Watermelon plant, muskmelon plant,
Your face on gardens looks.
Aha-aha-ehe-ihe.

RAIN

Today it's raining cats and dogs—
Poodles and tortoiseshells and tabbies.
Auntie went out, and had not gone long,
When there dropped on her head a huge ginger tom;
While, before he could get back inside the house,
A greyhound poured down on my Great Uncle Klaus,
Knocking him flat in the nearest puddle.
My pluvial pinnacle today, however,
Concerned a small, black cocker-spaniel.
When I opened my window he splashed from the sill,
Ears all a-droop like a weeping pussy-willow,
Sending a cloud-burst all over my pillow.

—Christine Crow

ONE MISTY MOISTY MORNING

One misty moisty morning
When cloudy was the weather,
I met with an old man
Clothed all in leather;
He was clothed all in leather
From his foot unto his chin,
Saying: "How de-do and how-de-do,
And how-de-do again."

—*Mother Goose*

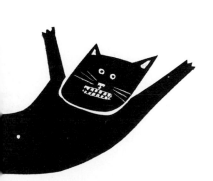

AN AWKWARD ARRANGEMENT

If I were rain and rain were me
We'd make an awkward company.
I'd make rain rise and never fall,
And no one would get wet at all
Excepting rain itself would get
A most absorbing kind of wet.
I don't expect rain will agree
That I be rain and it be me.

—Jane Yolen

A WRITING KIND OF DAY

It is raining today,
a writing kind of day.

Each word hits the page
like a drop in a puddle
and starts off a tiny circle

of trembling feeling

that expands from the source
and slowly fades away. . .

—Ralph Fletcher

SPRING THUNDER

Listen. The wind is still,
And far away in the night—
See! The uplands fill
With a running light.

Open the doors. It is warm;
And where the sky was clear—
Look! The head of a storm
That marches here!

Come under the trembling hedge—
Fast, although you fumble.
There! Did you hear the edge
Of winter crumble?

—Mark Van Doren

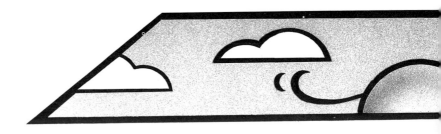

FROGS AND RAIN

Ranidae is what we call
the true frogs. On rainy days
we see among the waterwort and plantain
round eyes lined across
with spring water so clear
it is spotted only with leopard frogs and rain. . . .

and rain clears out the clouds.
Each drop brim full of hyacinth
can find the round egg-clouded pool. . . .

When enough sky has fallen
frogs sing among water stems,
blue buds spring.

—*Anna Kirwan-Vogel*

NOVEMBER RAIN

This autumn rainfall
   Is no shower
That freshens grass
   And brings the flower.

This rain is long
   And cold and gray,
Yet sleeping roots
   Are fed this way.

Trees and bushes,
   Nearly bare
Of leaves, now chains
   Of raindrops wear

Along each twig.
   Some clear beads fall.
A tree could never
   Hold them all.

—*Maud E. Uschold*

JUST WHEN I THOUGHT

It was a great day for clouds
and I wanted to tell someone
So I said it
a couple of times
and just when I thought
no one was listening
a raindrop fell
on me.

—*Anna Grossnickle Hines*

RAYS IN THE MIDDLE OF THE GREAT GREEN SEA

S U N

Dry August and warm
Doth harvest no harm.
—Mother Goose

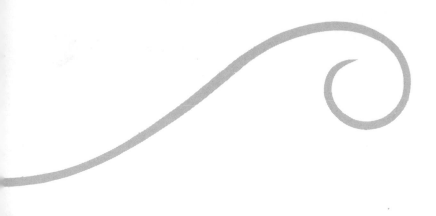

SUNFLAKES

If sunlight fell like snowflakes,
gleaming yellow and so bright,
we could build a sunman,
we could have a sunball fight,
we could watch the sunflakes
drifting in the sky.
We could go sleighing
in the middle of July
through sundrifts and sunbanks,
we could ride a sunmobile,
and we could touch sunflakes—
I wonder how they'd feel.

—*Frank Asch*

HYMN TO THE SUN

All the cattle are resting in the fields,
The trees and the plants are growing,
The birds flutter above the marshes,
Their wings uplifted in adoration,
And all the sheep are dancing,
All winged things are flying,
They live when you have shone on them.

The boats sail upstream and downstream alike,
Every highway is open because you dawn.
The fish in the river leap up in front of you,
Your rays are in the middle of the great green sea.

—*Anonymous, Ancient Egyptian*

SUN FOR BREAKFAST

Rise up and look
at pond, at brook.

Night now is gone.
Morning upon
her silver tray
is serving day.

All you who wake
up hungry: take!

—Norma Farber

AN INDIAN SUMMER DAY
ON THE PRAIRIE

In the Beginning
The sun is a huntress young,
The sun is a red, red joy,
The sun is an Indian girl,
Of the tribe of the Illinois.

Mid-Morning
The sun is a smoldering fire,
That creeps through the high gray plain,
And leaves not a bush of cloud
To blossom with flowers of rain.

Noon
The sun is a wounded deer,
That treads pale grass in the skies,
Shaking his golden horns,
Flashing his baleful eyes.

Sunset
The sun is an eagle old,
There in the windless west,
Atop of the spirit-cliffs
He builds him a crimson nest.

—*Vachel Lindsay*

SUMMER SUN

Great is the sun, and wide he goes
Through empty heaven without repose;
And in the blue and glowing days
More thick than rain he showers his rays.

Though closer still the blinds we pull
To keep the shady parlour cool,
Yet he will find a chink or two
To slip his golden fingers through.

The dusty attic spider-clad
He, through the keyhole, maketh glad;
And through the broken edge of tiles
Into the laddered hay-loft smiles.

Meantime his golden face around
He bares to all the garden ground,
And sheds a warm and glittering look
Among the ivy's inmost nook.

Above the hills, along the blue,
Round the bright air with footing true,
To please the child, to paint the rose,
The gardener of the World, he goes.

—Robert Louis Stevenson

I'LL TELL YOU HOW THE SUN ROSE

I'll tell you how the Sun rose—
A Ribbon at a time—
The Steeples swam in Amethyst—
The news, like Squirrels, ran—
The Hills untied their Bonnets—
The Bobolinks—begun—
Then I said softly to myself—
"That must have been the Sun!"
But how he set—I know not—
There seemed a purple stile
That little Yellow boys and girls
Were climbing all the while—
Till when they reached the other side,
A Dominie in Gray—
Put gently up the evening Bars—
And led the flock away—

—Emily Dickinson

IN FIELDS OF SUMMER

The sun rises,
The goldenrod blooms,
I drift in fields of summer,
My life is adrift in my body,
It shines in my heart and hands, in my teeth,
It shines up at the old crane
Who holds out his drainpipe of a neck
And creaks along in the blue,

And the goldenrod shines with its life, too,
And the grass, look,
The great field wavers and flakes,
The rumble of bumblebees keeps deepening,
A phoebe flutters up,
A lark bursts up all dew.

—*Galway Kinnell*

THE WAKING

I strolled across
An open field;
The sun was out;
Heat was happy.

This way! This way!
The wren's throat shimmered,
Either to other,
The blossoms sang.

The stones sang,
The little ones did,
And flowers jumped
Like small goats.

A ragged fringe
Of daisies waved;
I wasn't alone
In a grove of apples.

Far in the wood
A nestling sighed;
The dew loosened
Its morning smells.

I came where the river
Ran over stones:
My ears knew
An early joy.

And all the waters
Of all the streams
Sang in my veins
That summer day.

— *Theodore Roethke*

READING: SUMMER

Summer is with it,
  she's wild,
  she likes
  bare legs and cutoffs
  and camping
  and hikes;
  she dives in deep water,
  she wades in a stream,
  she guzzles cold drinks
  and she drowns in ice cream;
  she runs barefoot,
  she picnics,
  she fishes,
  digs bait,
  she pitches a tent
  and she stays up too late
  while she counts out the stars,

  swats mosquitoes and flies,
  hears crickets,
  smells pine trees,
  spies night-creature eyes;
  she rides bareback,
  goes sailing,
  plays tennis,
  climbs trees;
  she soaks in the sunshine;
  she gulps in a breeze;
  she tastes the warm air
  on the end of her tongue,
  and she falls asleep
  reading
  alone
  in the sun.

—*Myra Cohn Livingston*

VACATION SONG

Shine on me, oh, you gold, gold sun,
  Smile on me, oh, you blue, blue skies,
Sing, birds! and rouse the lazy breeze
  That, in the shadow, sleeping lies,
Calling, "Awaken! Slothful one
  And chase the yellow butterflies."

Frown if you will, you staid old trees,
  You cannot silence the birds and me;
You will sing yourself ere we leave you in peace,—
  Frown if you will but we shall see.
I'll pelt you with your own green leaves
  Till you echo the strains of our minstrelsy.

Oh, mower! All the world's at play,—
  Leave on the grass your sickle bright;
Come, and we'll dance a merry step
  With the birds and the leaves and the gold sunlight,
We'll dance till the shadows leave the hills
  And bring to the fields the quiet night.

—*Edna St. Vincent Millay*

I WILL BLOW YOU OUT

$\mathcal{W}$ I N D

No weather is ill,
If the wind be still
—Country wisdom

POEM

In a high wind the
leaves don't
fall but fly
straight out of the
tree like birds

—*A. R. Ammons*

WIND

Nobody knows
where the Wind goes—
it comes with a flutter
it goes with a gust,
it comes when it will
and it goes where it must
but—
where it goes,
nobody knows.

—*Ivy O. Eastwick*

NOTE

straw, feathers, dust—
little things

but if they all go one way,
that's the way the wind goes.

—William Stafford

THE WIND AND THE MOON

Said the Wind to the Moon,
"I will blow you out;
    You stare
    In the air
    Like a ghost in a chair
Always looking what I am about.
I hate to be watched—I'll blow you out."

—George Macdonald

WHO HAS SEEN THE WIND?

Who has seen the wind?
  Neither I nor you:
But when the leaves hang trembling,
  The wind is passing through.

Who has seen the wind?
  Neither you nor I:
But when the leaves bow down their heads,
  The wind is passing by.

—*Christina Rossetti*

IN THE BEGINNING

I know where the wind begins.
I saw it
as I lay on my back
under the old elm tree
in our front yard.

The air was still as still
when the elm began
to wave its leaves.
Just a flutter at first
then a little more
and *presto!*
came the breeze.

—*Anna Grossnickle Hines*

WHEN THE WIND

When the wind is in the east,
'Tis neither good for man or beast;
When the wind is in the north,
The skillful fisher goes not forth;
When the wind is in the south,
It blows the bait in the fishes' mouth;
When the wind is in the west,
Then 'tis at the very best.

—*Mother Goose*

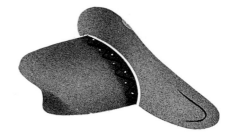

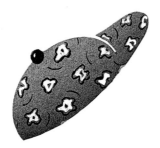

BLOW, BLOW, THOU WINTER WIND

Blow, blow, thou winter wind,
Thou art not so unkind
    As man's ingratitude;
Thy tooth is not so keen,
Because thou art not seen,
    Although thy breath be rude.
Heigh-ho! sing heigh-ho! unto the green holly;
Most friendship is feigning, most loving mere folly:
    Then, heigh-ho, the holly!
    This life is most jolly!

—*William Shakespeare*

THE WIND

I saw you toss the kites on high
And blow the birds about the sky;
And all around I heard you pass,
Like ladies' skirts across the grass—
    O wind, a-blowing all day long,
    O wind, that sings so loud a song!

I saw the different things you did,
But always you yourself you hid.
I felt you push, I heard you call,
I could not see yourself at all—
    O wind, a-blowing all day long,
    O wind, that sings so loud a song!

O you that are so strong and cold,
O blower, are you young or old?
Are you a beast of field and tree,
Or just a stronger child than me?
    O wind, a-blowing all day long,
    O wind, that sings so loud a song!

—*Robert Louis Stevenson*

WIND

Wind shouts, "Wait!
I want to play!"
Wind rides on pony,
scatters hay,
rattles the fence,
rat-a-tat-tat,
rat-a-tat-tat,
shakes the shutters,
open and shut,
open and shut!

Wind hurries our feet,
steals our hats,
whines alive
like twenty cats,
whips up leaves,
sweeps through poem,
shouts goodbye
and whistles home!

—*Irv Rosse (Rosenthal)*

ICICLE POPSICLES

S N O W

Snow, snow faster;
Ally-ally-blaster;
The old woman's plucking her geese,
Selling the feathers a penny apiece.
                    —Country wisdom

WINTER SONG

Snow, snow,
Shiver and blow.
Icicle Popsicles
            Drip-drip-and-dropsicles.
High-balling,
            low-balling,
Everyone's snowballing
And it keeps going
On snowing.

Snow, snow,
Shiver and blow.
Snowflakes and snowcakes
And pictures the frost makes.
Fingers and toes freeze
And snows make my nose sneeze
And it keeps going
On snowing.

—Jane Yolen

THE SNOW FALL

Quietness clings to the air.
Quietness gathers the bell
To a great distance.
Listen!
This is the snow.
This is the slow
Chime
The snow
Makes.
It encloses us.
Time in the snow is alone:
Time in the snow is at last,
Is past.

—Archibald MacLeish

DUST OF SNOW

The way a crow
Shook down on me
The dust of snow
From a hemlock tree

Has given my heart
A change of mood
And saved some part
Of a day I had rued.

—*Robert Frost*

CYNTHIA IN THE SNOW

IT SUSHES.
It hushes
The loudness in the road.
It flitter-twitters,
And laughs away from me.
It laughs a lovely whiteness,
And whitely whirs away,
To be
Some otherwhere,
Still white as milk or shirts.
So beautiful it hurts.

—*Gwendolyn Brooks*

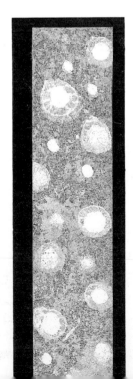

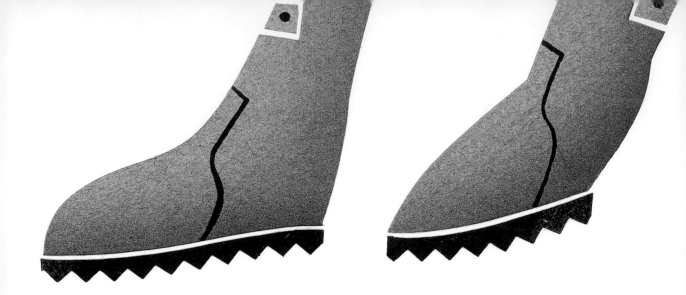

SNOW RHYME

White/sight,
Sledge/pledge,
Ice/nice,
Cold/bold,
Drift/rift,
Flake/lake,
Melt/felt,
Drop/hop,
Fall/ball—
Oh my dear white garden of winter rime,
How you grow on me like a poem.

—*Christine Crow*

WINTER MORNING

Winter is the king of showmen,
Turning tree stumps into snow men
And houses into birthday cakes
And spreading sugar over the lakes.
Smooth and clean and frost white
The world looks good enough to bite.
That's the season to be young,
Catching snowflakes on your tongue.

Snow is snowy when it's snowing
I'm sorry it's slushy when it's going.

—*Ogden Nash*

FIRST SNOW

There was just enough snow,
just enough white
for winter to write
on the ground
last night.

There was just enough white,
just enough snow,
for winter to write:
"I'm back. Hello."

—*Aileen Fisher*

ON TOP OF A HILL

I wish I lived
   on top of a hill
when the wind's in the North
      and the air is chill
      and the snow falls fast
      and the snow falls light
         all through the day
         and all through the night
            till everything's icy
               by morningtide
         and the way down the hill
               is one huge slide!

—*Ivy O. Eastwick*

WHITE FIELDS

In the wintertime we go
Walking in the fields of snow;

Where there is no grass at all;
Where the top of every wall,

Every fence and every tree,
Is as white as white can be.

Pointing out the way we came,
Every one of them the same—

All across the fields there be
Prints in silver filigree;

And our mothers always know,
By the footprints in the snow,

Where it is the children go.

—*James Stephens*

IT FELL IN THE CITY

It fell in the city,
It fell through the night,
And the black rooftops
All turned white.

Red fire hydrants
All turned white.
Blue police cars
All turned white.

Green garbage cans
All turned white.
Gray sidewalks
All turned white.

Yellow NO PARKING signs
All turned white
When it fell in the city
All through the night.

—*Eve Merriam*

ON LITTLE CAT FEET

F O G

Fog on the hill
Brings water to the mill.
Fog on the moor
Brings sun to the door.
— Country wisdom

FOG

Fog sneaks in,
Spongy and wet.

In gray mist
a silhouette
of eucalyptus
shrouded,
still,
disappears
into
the
hill.

—*Myra Cohn Livingston*

THE MIST AND ALL

I like the fall,
The mist and all.
I like the night owl's
Lonely call—
And wailing sound
Of wind around.

I like the gray
November day,
And bare, dead boughs
That coldly sway
Against my pane.
I like the rain.

I like to sit
And laugh at it—
And tend
My cozy fire a bit.
I like the fall—
The mist and all.

—*Dixie Willson*

FOG

The fog comes
on little cat feet.

It sits looking
over harbor and city
on silent haunches
and then moves on.

—Carl Sandburg

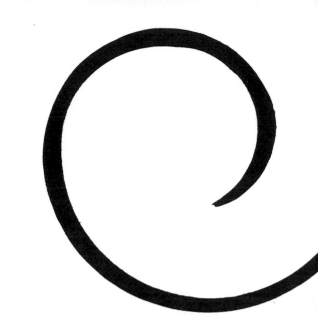

NOTE TO CARL SANDBURG

Come and see the long gray trail
Left here by the garden snail.
That's the foot on which the fog creeps
Late at night when all the world sleeps.

—Jane Yolen

WINDSHIELD WIPER

fog smog	fog smog
tissue paper	tissue paper
clear the blear	clear the smear
fog more	fog more
splat splat	downpour
rubber scraper	rubber scraper
overshoes	macintosh
bumbershoot	muddle on
slosh through	slosh through
drying up	drying up
sky lighter	sky lighter
nearly clear	nearly clear

clearing clearing veer
clear here clear

—Eve Merriam

FOG

Did the spiders
    come out last night to
    play?
Did they spin and spin
    the night
    away?
Is that why the world
    is cobweb gray
    today?

—Lilian Moore

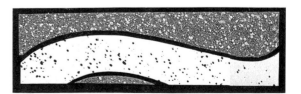

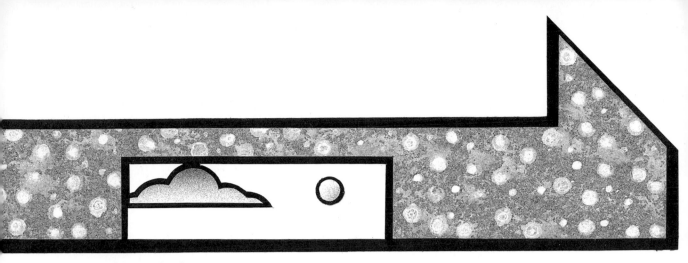

IN THE FOG

Stand still.
The fog wraps you up
and no one can find you.

Walk.
The fog opens up
to let you through
and closes behind you.

—*Lilian Moore*

RIVER

A delicate fuzz of fog
like mold, or moss,
all across the river
in this early light.
Another day, I might
have still been sleeping.

What a pity. How the stars
and seas and rivers
in their fragile lace of fog
go on without us
morning after morning,
year after year.
And we disappear.

—*Pat Schneider*

Acknowledgments

Every effort has been made to trace the ownership of all copyrighted material and to secure the necessary permissions to reprint these selections. In the event of any question arising as to the use of any material, the editor and publisher, while expressing regret for any inadvertent error, will be happy to make the necessary correction in future printings.

"Poem" from DIVERSIFICATIONS, Poems by A.R. Ammons. Copyright © 1975 by A.R. Ammons. Used by permission of W.W. Norton & Company, Inc.

"Sunflakes" from COUNTRY PIE by Frank Asch. Copyright © 1979 by Frank Asch. Used by permission of Greenwillow Books, a division of William Morrow & Company, Inc.

"Cynthia in the Snow" from BRONZEVILLE BOYS AND GIRLS by Gwendolyn Brooks. Copyright © 1956 by Gwendolyn Brooks Blakely. Used by permission of HarperCollins Publishers, Inc.

"Rain Sizes" from THE REASON FOR THE PELICAN by John Ciardi. Copyright © 1959 by John Ciardi. Used by permission of Mrs. Judith Ciardi.

"Rain" and "Snow Rhyme" by Christine Crow. Copyright © 1992 by Christine Crow. Used by permission of the author.

"I'll Tell You How the Sun Rose" by Emily Dickinson. Used by permission of Harvard University Press.

"On Top of a Hill" copyright © 1976 and "Wind" copyright © 1980, both by Ivy O. Eastwick. Used by permission of HIGHLIGHTS FOR CHILDREN.

"Sun for Breakfast" by Norma Farber. Used by permission of Thomas Farber.

"First Snow" from RUNNY DAYS, SUNNY DAYS by Aileen Fisher. Copyright © 1958 by Aileen Fisher. Used by permission of the author.

"A Writing Kind of Day" from WATER PLANET by Ralph Fletcher. Used by permission of the author.

"Dust of Snow" by Robert Frost. From THE POETRY OF ROBERT FROST, edited by Edward Connery Latham. Copyright © 1923, 1969 by Holt, Rinehart and Winston, Inc. Copyright © 1951 by Robert Frost. Used by permission of Henry Holt and Company.

"In the Beginning" and "Just When I Thought" by Anna Grossnickle Hines. Copyright © 1992 by Anna Grossnickle Hines. Used by permission of Curtis Brown, Ltd.

"April Rain Song" from THE DREAM KEEPER AND OTHER POEMS by Langston Hughes. Copyright © 1932 by Alfred A. Knopf, Inc., renewed 1960 by Langston Hughes. Used by permission of Alfred A. Knopf, Inc.

"In Fields of Summer" from FLOWER HERDING ON MOUNT MONADNOCK by Galway Kinnell. Copyright © 1964 by Galway Kinnell. Used by permission of Houghton Mifflin Company. All rights reserved.

"Frogs and Rain" by Anna Kirwan-Vogel. Copyright © 1992 by Anna Kirwan-Vogel. Used by permission of Curtis Brown, Ltd.

"Fog" from REMEMBERING AND OTHER POEMS by Myra Cohn Livingston. Copyright © 1989 by Myra Cohn Livingston. Used by permission of Margaret K. McElderry Books, an imprint of Macmillan Publishing Company.

"Reading: Summer" from REMEMBERING AND OTHER POEMS by Myra Cohn Livingston. Copyright © 1989 by Myra Cohn Livingston. Used by permission of Marian Reiner.

"The Snow Fall" from ACT FIVE AND OTHER POEMS by Archibald MacLeish. Copyright © 1948 by Archibald MacLeish. Used by permission of Houghton Mifflin Company.

"Chatterbox, The Rain" by Beverly McLoughland. Copyright © 1991 by Beverly McLoughland. Used by permission of HIGHLIGHTS FOR CHILDREN.

Index

by AUTHOR, *Title*, and First Line